THIS BOOK BELONGS TO:

_____

_____

_____

meomi

WOULD LIKE TO DEDICATE THIS BOOK TO FRIENDS BIG AND SMALL

I like apples!

I play video games.

Yeti crabs are cool.

I like lentils!

I make smoothies.

Manatees are cute.

This book was written and illustrated by MEOMI
(the not-secret pen name of Vicki Wong & Michael C. Murphy).
Learn more about them at www.meomi.com

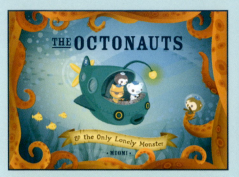

First published in paperback in Great Britain
by HarperCollins Children's Books in 2014

10 9 8 7 6

ISBN: 978-0-00-828329-2

HarperCollins Children's Books is a division of HarperCollins Publishers Ltd.

Text and illustrations copyright © MEOMI Design Inc.:
Vicki Wong and Michael Murphy 2014

Visit our website at www.harpercollins.co.uk

Printed and bound in China

I LOVE GETTING MY CLAWS ON A GOOD BOOK!

THE OCTONAUTS

& the Growing Goldfish

• MEOMI •

HarperCollins *Children's Books*

It was a sunny morning under the golden ocean when...

Shellington Sea Otter was digging for fossils.

Professor Inkling was listening to music.

Captain Barnacles Bear was building a model.

Tweak Bunny was playing her banjo.

FISH SOUNDS

Kwazii Kitten was swabbing the decks.

Peso Penguin was examining a patient.

Tunip the Vegimal was eating breakfast.

Dashi Dog was urgently calling the Octopod!

KAP'N KELP

100% KELP

FREE!

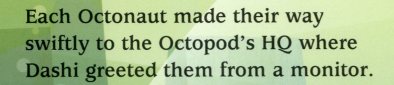

Each Octonaut made their way swiftly to the Octopod's HQ where Dashi greeted them from a monitor.

"I was taking photos in a nearby park when I met Dunkie," she said. "He's a goldfish who's grown so much, he doesn't fit in his pond any more. We need to move him quickly!"

"This sounds like a chance to try out my new invention," Tweak suggested. "The GUP-G! I built it to travel in water *and* on land, just like a giant salamander."

The ship had sturdy legs for walking on ground and a special tank for carrying large creatures. With no time to spare, the GUP was loaded with kelp cakes and equipment, and the Octonauts set off for the park.

At first, I was the same size as all the other goldfish.

me↗

The crew journeyed up on to the shore, through a forest, and over rolling hills. When they reached Dunkie's pond, the troubled goldfish shared his story with the crew...

But then I got bigger...

AND BIGGER

Now, there's not enough room for me here!

OR US!!!

Captain Barnacles comforted their new friend. "Everyone is different. Some of us grow a little and some grow a lot," he said. "We'll help you find a larger pond – one with space for you to swim!"

Just then, an old koi fish spoke up. "I've heard tales of a hidden ocean where giants swim! To find it, you must head east and follow the Rocky River to where it meets the clouds."

The Octonauts thanked the wise koi and set off on their quest.
As they travelled, Dunkie continued to grow. When they finally
reached the river, he was too big even for the ship!

In the water, Peso came out to measure Dunkie's astonishing size.
Shellington studied his shimmering scales and noted that they were
looking more and more like armoured plates.

Further down the river, the currents suddenly turned into rapids and waves crashed wildly against the tall banks. Dunkie and the Octonauts were jostled left and right.

"We can't take any more of this!" Captain Barnacles shouted as he struggled to steer. "I'm losing control of the GUP-G!"

Ahead, the river seemed to disappear into the sky. It was a...

"Yargh! We're going to crash!" Kwazii cried as the GUP fell over the edge towards the sharp rocks below.

But, at the last moment, strong jaws clamped on to the ship.

Dunkie twisted around with all his might and pushed the Octonauts away from the rocks...

... and through
the rushing water.

YAY!

The crew found themselves floating in the
calm of a tunnel *behind* the waterfall.
Dunkie had saved them!

Nautiloid

Acanthodes

Wiwaxia

Platyceramus

Hemicyclaspis

Plectronoceras

Further ahead, the tunnel opened on to a vast,
underground ocean lit by dazzling crystals.
The crew gasped in awe. Gigantic fish swam slowly
before them and large plants covered the sea bed.
Was this the ocean of giants?

Onchopristis

Hallucigenia

Opabinia

Horseshoe crab

Trilobite

Plesiosaurus

Parexus

Ammonite

Bichir

Cautiously, the Octonauts left their ship to explore.
"These fish look familiar," Shellington said excitedly.
"They remind me of the fossils I've been studying!"

Super! A Coelacanth!

Hello! I'm a Henodus!

Terrific! A Pteraspis!

An amazing Anomalocaris!

Oh my!
A Megalodon!!

While the crew were busy
spotting creatures,
Dunkie had a surprise of his own
– giant fish that looked
just like him!

Professor Inkling pulled out his book to explain. "Living fossils are plants and animals that haven't changed for millions of years – sometimes since the time of the dinosaurs!"

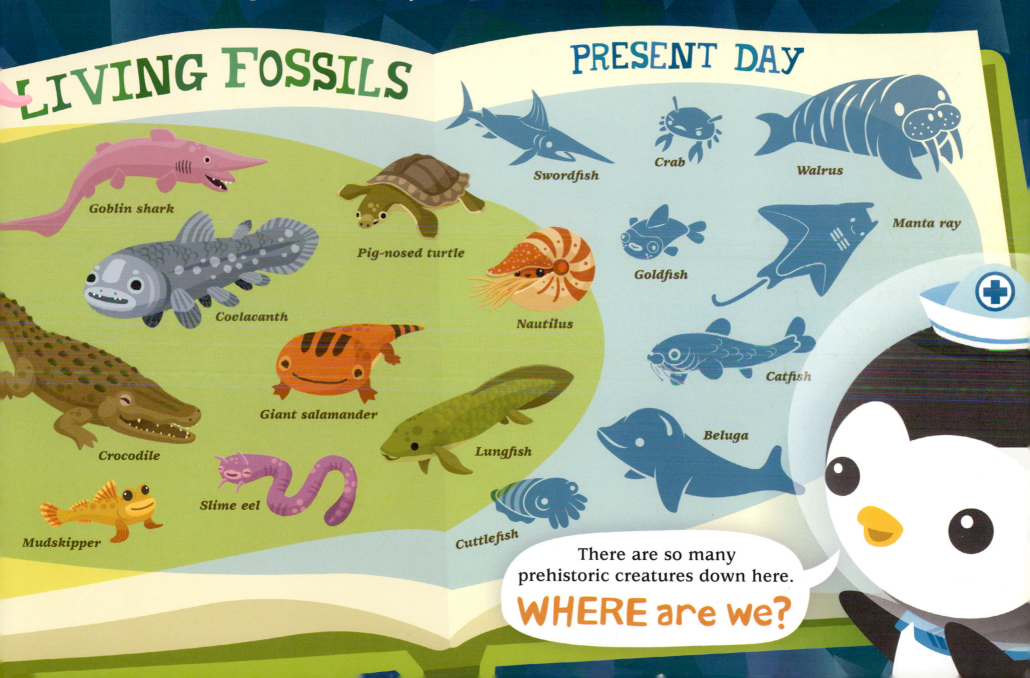

LIVING FOSSILS

PRESENT DAY

Goblin shark

Coelacanth

Pig-nosed turtle

Nautilus

Crocodile

Giant salamander

Lungfish

Mudskipper

Slime eel

Cuttlefish

Swordfish

Crab

Walrus

Manta ray

Goldfish

Catfish

Beluga

There are so many prehistoric creatures down here.
WHERE are we?

NOT THAT FAR

FAR

OTTO

Dashi studied her Octo-map...
"According to the locator, we're
right where we began!" she gasped.
"This ocean is under
Dunkie's pond in the park –
just far... far... far... below!"

"Dunkie's egg must have drifted through
a crack in the rock and up to the
pond above," Shellington suggested.

FARTHER

FARTHEST

Later, as new friends big and small swam up to greet them,
Dunkie waved his fins and tossed his tail happily.
"There's plenty of room for me here!" he said.

WELCOME DUNKIE

The Octonauts stayed on for a giant party.
Everyone enjoyed humongous kelp cakes and
drank gigantic cups of kelp juice.

When it was time to head back to the Octopod,
Captain Barnacles asked Dunkie, "Will you be all right here?
There are a lot of *really* big fish around..."
"Don't worry about me," Dunkie answered cheerfully,
"I'm still growing!"

MEET THE OCTONAUTS!

CAPTAIN BARNACLES

Captain Barnacles is a brave polar bear extraordinaire and the leader of the Octonauts crew. He's always the first to rush in and help whenever there's a problem. In addition to exploring, Barnacles enjoys playing his accordion and writing in his captain's log.

LIEUTENANT KWAZII

Kwazii is a daredevil orange kitten with a mysterious pirate past. He's never one to turn down an adventure and he loves travelling to exotic places. His favourite hobbies include long baths, racing the GUP-B, and general swashbuckling.

NURSE PESO

Peso is the medic for the team. He's an expert at bandaging and always carries his medical kit with him in case of emergencies. He's not too fond of scary things, but if a creature is hurt or in danger, Peso can be the bravest Octonaut of all!

DR SHELLINGTON

Dr Shellington is a nerdy sea otter scientist who loves doing field research and working in his lab. He's easily distracted by rare plants and animals, but his knowledge of the ocean is a big help in Octonaut missions.

TWEAK BUNNY

Tweak is the engineer for the Octonauts. She designed and built the Octopod along with the team's growing fleet of GUPs. Tweak enjoys tinkering and inventing tools that sometimes work in unexpected ways.

DASHI DOG

Dashi is a sweet dachshund who oversees operations in the Octopod HQ and launch bay. She programmes the computers and manages all ship traffic. She's also the Octonauts' official photographer and enjoys taking photos of undersea life.

PROFESSOR INKLING

Professor Inkling is a brilliant Dumbo octopus oceanographer. He founded the Octonauts with the intention of furthering underwater research and preservation. Because of his delicate, big brain, he prefers to help the team from his library in the Octopod.

TUNIP THE VEGIMAL

Tunip is one of many Vegimals; special sea creatures that are part vegetable and part animal. They speak their own language that only Shellington can understand (sometimes!) Vegimals help out around the Octopod and love to bake: kelp cakes, kelp cookies, kelp soufflé...